This book belongs to

Austin Strougo

A Read-Aloud Storybook

Adapted by Julie Michaels

Illustrated by Judith H. Clarke, Denise Shimabukuro,
Dominio Dai, Adrienne Brown, and Brent Ford

Random House 🏠 New York

Copyright © 2000 by Disney Enterprises, Inc. All rights reserved under International and Pan-American Copyright
Conventions. Published in the United States by Random House, Inc., New York, and simultaneously in Canada by
Random House of Canada Limited, Toronto, in conjunction with Disney Enterprises, Inc. RANDOM HOUSE
and colophon are registered trademarks of Random House, Inc. Originally published by Mouse Works in 2000.
Printed in the United States of America   ISBN: 0-7364-1000-7
First Random House Edition May 2001

www.randomhouse.com/kids/disney

The Discovery

Long, long ago, a lemur named Plio made an exciting discovery. "Dad, get over here!" she cried.

The strange egg she'd found began to crack. Inside was a baby dinosaur!

"It's a cold-blooded monster from across the sea," warned Plio's father, Yar.

"It looks like a baby to me," said Plio. And so the dinosaur began his life on Lemur Island.

The lemurs named the dinosaur Aladar, and watched with amazement as the tiny baby grew into a giant iguanodon!

Friendly Aladar loved his lemur family. Plio's daughter, Suri, was just like a little sister to him.

10

One day Plio called the young lemurs: it was time for the courtship ritual.

Lemurs swung through the vines of the Ritual Tree, choosing partners.

But Aladar's friend Zini got hopelessly tangled! "You always have next year," Aladar said kindly.

But Aladar would never find one of his own kind on Lemur Island. "If only there was someone on the island for you," Plio told him.

The Fireball

Suddenly a deep stillness fell over the island.
"Something's wrong," Yar said grimly.
"Aladar, where's Suri?" cried Plio.

Across the sea, a huge meteor had crashed to the earth. Now an enormous wave of fire and water was roaring toward Lemur Island!

Aladar raced across the island, carrying Plio, Suri, Yar, and Zini. Finally he reached a cliff at the edge of the island. With the giant Fireball right behind him, Aladar plunged toward the sea below!

Aladar swam his friends toward the mainland. Their beautiful island home had been destroyed.

Through a cloud of gathering dust, the small group saw a herd of . . . dinosaurs! "Look at all the Aladars!" cried Suri.

Aladar and the lemurs joined the Herd. They met two of the slower dinosaurs, Baylene and Eema.

"The Herd is marching to the Nesting Grounds to have their babies," explained Eema. The trip was difficult: the Fireball had changed much of the land.

Aladar stopped the Herd leader, Kron. "Maybe you could slow it down a bit?" he asked. Baylene and Eema could barely keep up.

"Let the weak set the pace?" Kron thought Aladar was joking.

Kron and his scout, Bruton, knew that the Herd needed to find water to survive. And they needed to stay ahead of their enemies, the savage carnotaurs.

Aladar struggled to help Eema and Baylene keep pace with the Herd. At last Eema called out, "The lake! It's just over that hill!"

But the Fireball had turned the lake into a dry bed of sunbaked rocks and bones.

Aladar had an idea! If he dug a hole, he might find water beneath the sand.

"Water!" he cried. The Herd stampeded toward the water hole.

Later that night, Aladar noticed Suri trying to coax two small dinosaurs from a cave.

"The little Aladars haven't had anything to drink," she explained.

As Aladar was showing the dinosaurs how to get water, Kron's sister, Neera, approached.

Neera thought Aladar was kind to look after the little dinosaurs.

"If we watch out for each other," Aladar explained, "we all stand a better chance of getting to your Nesting Grounds."

Survival

On a nearby hill, a wounded Bruton brought bad news: carnotaurs were coming!

"Move the Herd out—double time!" thundered Kron.

Kron forced Neera along with the Herd. Aladar stayed behind with his slower friends.

As night came on, his little group realized they couldn't find the Herd. But they did find Bruton—the Herd had left him behind, too.

43

When the rain began, the friends took refuge in a cave. Even Bruton joined them. To his surprise, Plio gently nursed his wounds.

Suddenly the carnotaurs entered the cave and
attacked Aladar! Bruton pushed into the battle.

"I'll hold them off," Bruton told Aladar. Bruton got rid of the carnotaurs—but did not survive the battle.

Aladar and his friends walked deeper into the cave, hoping to find another way out.

Then Zini smelled fresh air! They began digging at the rocks, trying to break through to the outside.

But the digging wasn't working: Aladar
began to give up. "You gave us hope," Baylene
told him. "And I'm going to go on believing it!"
The group gave a big push—they broke through
the wall of rock and into the Nesting Grounds!

53

54

The Herd was not in the valley.

Eema looked at a rocky landslide. "That's the way we used to get in," she said worriedly. Aladar knew he had to go back and show the Herd the new way to the Nesting Grounds.

Aladar found Kron urging the Herd over the dangerous landslide. "There's a safer way!" he called.

Kron thought Aladar was trying to take over leadership of the Herd. He knocked Aladar to the ground.

Neera knocked her brother away from Aladar. When she and Aladar began walking to the cave, the Herd followed.

Then a carnotaur appeared! "If we scatter, he'll pick us off," Aladar told the Herd. "Stand together!"

The carnotaur decided to attack the one dinosaur that stood alone—Kron.

Neera and Aladar ran to help Kron. But they were too late.

Then the carnotaur turned on Neera. But she
and Aladar defeated the beast.
Now the Herd could move on.

Some weeks later, Aladar and Neera watched their first baby hatch.

"Oh, oh, happy day!" cheered Eema.

At last the friends had found a new home.

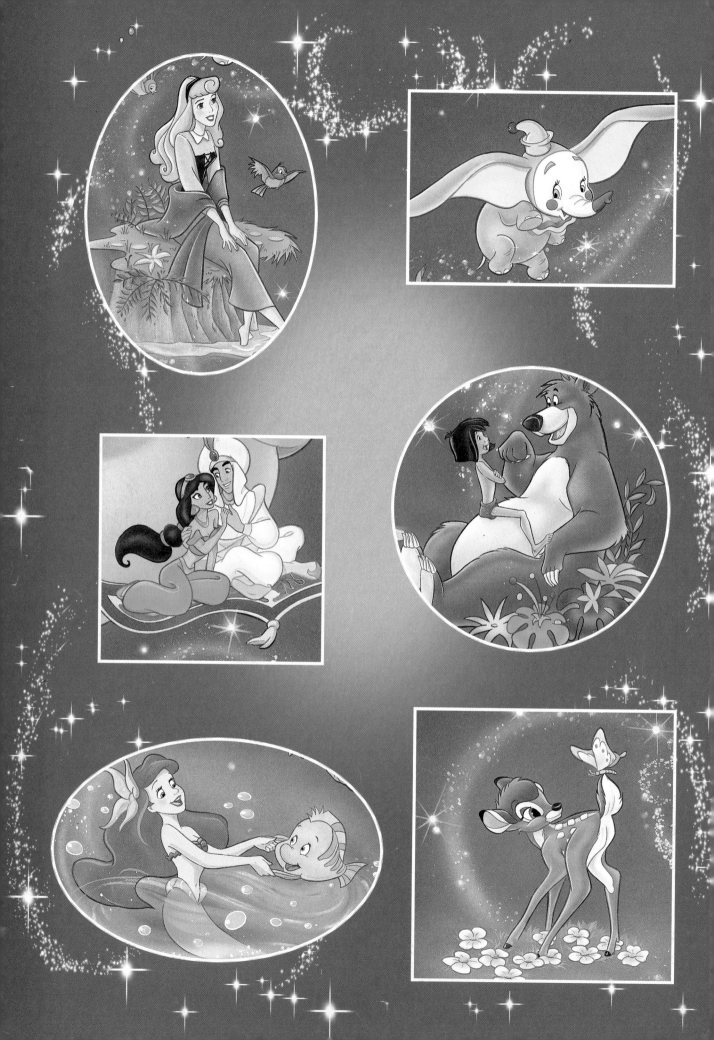